Tom and Ricky

and the

Man From Australia

Bob Wright

High Noon Books
Novato, California

Cover Design: Nancy Peach
Illustrations: Herb Heidinger

Glossary: garage, worth, bang, oranges, window

International Standard Book Number: 0-87879-368-2

10 09 08 07 06 05 04 03
15 14 13 12 11 10

You'll enjoy all the High Noon Books.
Write for a free full list of titles.

Contents

CHAPTER 1

A Hot July Afternoon

It was a hot July afternoon. Tom went over to Ricky's house on his bike. Ricky was in the yard with his dog Patches.

"Hi, Tom. Want to do something?" Ricky asked.

"I can't. Mr. Fall asked me to help him clean out his garage. I said I would. Want to help me?" Tom asked.

"OK. Wait here. I have to tell my mom." Ricky ran into the house.

"What's your hurry, Ricky?" his mom said.

"Tom is going to clean out Mr. Fall's garage. He wants me to help him. Is that OK with you?"

"Yes. I think it will be all right," she answered.

The phone rang.

"Get the phone before you go, Ricky," his mom said.

Ricky picked up the phone. "Hello," he said.

"Hi, Ricky. This is Eddie. Can you come over to my house?" Eddie asked.

"What do you want to do?" Ricky asked.

"Mr. Little has some very old stamps at his store. They are worth a lot of money. I want to see them. Want to go?" Eddie asked.

2

"I can't. Tom and I are going over to Mr. Fall's house," Ricky said.

"Why are you going over there?" Eddie asked.

"To help Mr. Fall clean out his garage. I'll call you later," Ricky said.

Ricky ran back into the yard.

"Ready to go?" Tom asked.

"Yes," Ricky answered.

"Who was on the phone?" Tom asked.

"It was Eddie. He wanted us to go to see some very old stamps," Ricky said.

"What did you tell him?" Tom asked.

"That we were helping Mr. Fall," Ricky said.

"Maybe we can go with him later," Tom said.

Ricky got on his bike.

Patches jumped up. He wagged his tail at the boys.

Ricky said, "Stay here, Patches. You can't go with us."

Tom said, "Yes, Patches. Stay here. You can't dig holes in Mr. Fall's yard. He wouldn't like it."

Patches barked and barked. He was not happy. He didn't like to be left behind.

Tom and Ricky went very fast on their bikes. They were in a hurry to get to Mr. Fall's house.

It was not long before they were there. Mr. Fall lived across the street from Little's Stamp Store.

"Why would Mr. Fall close all of the windows?"

"I bet Eddie is at the stamp store," Ricky said.

They got off their bikes and locked them. Then they walked to the house.

"That's funny," Tom said.

"What is?" asked Ricky.

"All of the windows are closed. It's hot today. Why would Mr. Fall close all of the windows?" Tom asked.

"I don't know. Let's ask him," Ricky said.

CHAPTER 2

Closed Windows

Tom banged on Mr. Fall's front door. Mr. Fall didn't have a door bell. Tom and Ricky waited. Then Tom banged again. Still no one came.

"Do you think Mr. Fall went somewhere?" Ricky asked.

"No. He must be here. He told me to come this afternoon. I hope he isn't sick," Tom said.

"Maybe he didn't hear you. Try again," Ricky said.

Tom banged on the door a few more times.

"I hear someone coming. It must be Mr. Fall," Tom said.

A man opened the door. It wasn't Mr. Fall. The man looked mad. "Get lost, boys," the man said.

"Where is Mr. Fall?" Tom asked.

"I told you to get lost," the man yelled at them. Now he looked very mad.

"I'm Tom. Mr. Fall wants me to clean out his garage this afternoon. My friend Ricky came with me to help," Tom said.

The man tried to be nice. "Boys, I'm sorry I yelled at you. I didn't know you were here to help my dad." But he didn't move so they could go in the house.

Tom was very surprised. "Are you Mr. Fall's son?" he asked.

"Yes, I am. My name is Clay," the man answered.

Tom said, "But your dad told me that you live in Australia."

The man's face turned red. "I do live in Australia. I'm here to see my dad. I'll be here only a few days. Then I have to go back to Australia," Clay said.

"Mr. Fall didn't say you were coming," Tom said.

"He didn't know. I wanted to surprise him," Clay said.

"That must have surprised him," Tom said.

"I bet it's fun to live in Australia. I know you could tell us a lot about it," Ricky said.

"Yes, but I'm busy now," Clay said. He started to close the door.

"Wait. Aren't you going to let us in? We're here to help your dad clean out his garage," Ricky said.

"You can't come in. And you can't clean out the garage this afternoon. My dad is very sick," Clay said.

"Is he going to be OK?" Tom asked.

"Yes. He'll be OK in a few days. You must go now. I have to take care of my dad." Then Clay closed the door.

Tom and Ricky walked back to their bikes.

Ricky said, "I don't like him very much. He isn't as nice as Mr. Fall."

"No, he isn't. I wish we had talked to Mr. Fall. I hope he's going to be OK," Tom said.

"I hope so, too. Maybe we should tell my mom that he's sick," Ricky said.

"Good idea! Let's hurry and tell her. Then we can see Eddie," Tom said.

Tom got on his bike. Ricky got on his bike.

Ricky said, "Wait, Tom. I just thought of something."

"What?" Tom asked.

"Mr. Little is going to get some very old stamps at his store today. Mr. Little told Eddie they are worth a lot of money," Ricky said.

"Really?" Tom asked.

"Yes. The stamps may be there now. I'd like to see them. Maybe Eddie is there, too. Do you want to stop by the store now?" Ricky asked.

"No. Let's stop by there later," Tom answered. Then he looked back at Mr. Fall's house. "I still think it's funny."

"What's funny?" Ricky asked.

"That all of the windows are closed. Why would Mr. Fall close all the windows on a hot July day?" Tom asked.

"I don't know. Maybe he's cold," Ricky said.

"Very funny, Ricky," Tom said.

CHAPTER 3

Soup and Oranges

It didn't take Tom and Ricky long to get back to Ricky's house.

"Ricky, is that you?" his mother called out.

"Yes, it is," Ricky answered.

"What are you doing back home so soon? Did you clean Mr. Fall's garage that fast?" she asked.

"We can't this afternoon. Mr. Fall is sick," Ricky answered.

Ricky's mom said, "I'm sorry to hear that."

Tom said, "We don't know what's wrong. His son just said he was sick."

Ricky's mom looked surprised. "I thought his son lived in Australia," she said.

"He does. He wanted to surprise his father. He'll be here only a few days. Mr. Fall didn't know he was coming," Ricky said.

Tom said, "We don't know what's wrong. His son just said he was sick. He wouldn't let us see him or talk to him."

"I wish we could help Mr. Fall get well," Ricky said.

"Maybe you can," Ricky's mom said. "You can take him some chicken soup and some oranges. I'll get them for you."

"That's a good idea. Then maybe we can see Mr. Fall. I want to be sure he's OK. I didn't like his son very much. He didn't seem very nice," Ricky said.

"He isn't as nice as Mr. Fall. And he was in a hurry to get rid of us," Tom said.

"Maybe he had to go take care of his dad," Ricky's mom said.

Ricky said, "That's what he told us."

"We saw something funny when we were there," Tom said.

"You saw something funny? What was that?" Ricky's mom asked.

"Mr. Fall had all of his windows closed," Tom said.

"That is funny. It's very hot today," Ricky's mom said. She put a jar of soup in a small bag. She gave it to Tom. Then she gave Ricky a bag of oranges.

"Mr. Fall will like those," Tom said.

She said, "Tell Mr. Fall that I hope he gets well."

"OK. We'll take these to Mr. Fall's house. Then we're going to see Eddie. We'll take Patches with us," Ricky said.

They went outside and got on their bikes.

Ricky said, "Come on, Patches. You can go with us this time."

CHAPTER 4

The Man Gets Mad

Patches ran next to the boys on their way to Mr. Fall's house. He was glad to be with them.

Soon they got to Mr. Fall's house. The windows were still closed. Patches ran with the boys to the front door.

Ricky said, "Stay with us, Patches. Don't dig any holes in Mr. Fall's yard."

Tom banged on the door. No one came. Tom banged louder. Then he banged a few more times.

17

Clay opened the door. He looked very mad.

"Why are you two back? What do you want now?"

Ricky said, "My mom sent some oranges and soup for your dad."

18

Patches barked at the man. He didn't like him at all.

"Patches! Sit down," Tom said.

Ricky said, "My mom sent some oranges and soup for your dad." He gave the man the bag of oranges.

Tom gave Clay the bag with the jar of soup. "Can we see Mr. Fall?" he asked.

"No! I need to take care of my dad. He needs his rest. Now get lost!" Clay started to close the door.

"Wait," Tom said.

"What now?" the man said.

Tom said, "You should open the windows. It's very hot today."

"This isn't very hot at all. You should be in Australia now. It's a lot hotter there in July than it is here. Now get lost. My father needs his rest." Then Clay closed the door.

"I hope he doesn't stay here long," Tom said.

"I'm glad I'm not in Australia now. I wouldn't want to be any hotter," Ricky said.

Tom said, "I'm worried about Mr. Fall. I wish we had talked to him. I hope he's OK."

Ricky said, "Let's come by tomorrow and ask about him. Maybe we can see him then."

"OK. Now let's go over to Eddie's house," Tom said.

"Come on, Patches," Ricky said.

CHAPTER 5

Hot in Australia?

Eddie opened the door as soon as he heard Patches. He knew that Tom and Ricky were there.

"Come on in," he called.

"Did you see the old stamps at Little's Stamp Store?" Ricky asked.

"No. I've been playing video games. I wanted to wait for you and Tom. It didn't take you long to clean out Mr. Fall's garage," Eddie said.

"We didn't get to help him. He's sick," Tom said.

"What's wrong with him?" Eddie asked.

Ricky said, "We don't know. We didn't get to talk to him."

"Then how do you know he's sick?" Eddie asked.

"His son told us," Tom answered.

Eddie said, "I didn't know Mr. Fall had a son. I thought he lived by himself."

"He does. But his son is here for a few days," Tom said.

"Where did his son come from?" Eddie asked.

"Australia," Ricky answered.

"Australia? That's a long way from here," Eddie said.

"It sure is. I looked it up on a map," Ricky said.

"Well, I'm glad you didn't have to clean out the garage this afternoon. Now we can all do something," Eddie said.

"Like what?" Tom asked.

Eddie said, "We could play a video game. Or we could go to the stamp store."

"It's too hot to stay inside," Ricky said.

"We saw something funny at Mr. Fall's house," Tom said.

"What?" Eddie asked.

"Tell him, Tom," Ricky said.

Tom told Eddie about the windows being closed.

Eddie said, "Why didn't you tell Mr. Fall's son to open the windows?"

"Tom did. But the man said we should be in Australia now. That it's hotter there in July than it is here," Ricky said.

Eddie looked surprised. "The man said it's hotter in Australia in July than here?" he said.

"Yes," Ricky answered.

"Then he isn't really from Australia," Eddie said.

"How do you know?" Tom asked.

Eddie said, "It's hot here in July. But it's winter in Australia in July."

"Are you sure?" Ricky asked.

"Yes, I'm sure," Eddie answered.

Tom and Ricky looked at each other. Then Tom said, "That man couldn't be from Australia."

"But Mr. Fall's son lives in Australia," Ricky said.

"So that man isn't Mr. Fall's son. But who is he?" Tom asked.

"I don't know. Now I'm worried. I think the man may have hurt Mr. Fall," Ricky said.

"What should we do? We can't just sit here," Tom said.

"Let's call Sergeant Collins. He'll know what to do," Ricky said.

Eddie handed Ricky the phone. "Here. You call him."

Ricky called the police station. Another policeman answered. Sergeant Collins wasn't there.

Ricky said, "Please tell Sergeant Collins that his friend Ricky called. I must talk to him right away. Please ask him to meet me at Eddie's house.

The policeman said he would tell Sergeant Collins.

CHAPTER 6

Sergeant Collins Comes

Ricky put down the phone.

"What did the policeman say?" Eddie asked.

"That he would tell Sergeant Collins I need to see him," Ricky said.

Tom said, "I hope Sergeant Collins gets here soon. Let's wait for him outside."

Very soon the boys saw a police car coming down the street. It stopped in front of Eddie's house. Sergeant Collins got out of the car. They all ran to meet him.

"We sure are glad to see you," Ricky said.

"Hello, boys. What's wrong? Why did you want me to come?" the Sergeant asked.

"Tell me everything you know," Sergeant Collins said to the boys.

Tom said, "We're worried about a friend of ours. His name is Mr. Fall. He lives a few streets away from here."

"He lives in an old house across the street from Little's Stamp Store," Ricky said.

Sergeant Collins asked, "Why are you worried about your friend?"

"We think he may be hurt," Ricky answered.

Tom said, "We think a strange man may have hurt him."

"Tell me everything you know," Sergeant Collins said to the boys.

"Mr. Fall asked me to help him clean out his garage this afternoon. Ricky and I went over to his house," Tom said.

"Go on," the Sergeant said.

"I banged on the front door many times. Then a man answered. But it wasn't Mr. Fall. I never saw that man before," Tom said.

Ricky said, "He said he was Mr. Fall's son. He wouldn't let us inside the house. He said Mr. Fall was sick."

"But he couldn't be Mr. Fall's son," Eddie said.

"How do you know that?" Sergeant Collins asked.

"Because Mr. Fall's son lives in Australia," Tom said.

Sergeant Collins said, "He could have come here to see his dad."

"That's what he told us. But we know he isn't from Australia," Ricky said.

"How do you know that?" the Sergeant asked.

Tom said, "All of Mr. Fall's windows were closed. I told the man he should open them because it's very hot today. He said it's hotter in Australia in July than here."

Then Eddie said, "But that isn't so. I read about Australia. Australia has its winter in July."

Ricky said, "So this man couldn't have lived in Australia. That's why we know he isn't Mr. Fall's son. We hope you can find out who he really is."

"And if Mr. Fall is all right," Tom said.

Sergeant Collins looked worried. "I'm glad you called me, boys. I think I should find out who this man is. Mr. Fall may need some help."

CHAPTER 7

More Policemen Come

Sergeant Collins got in his car and called the police station. He asked for some policemen to meet him at Eddie's house. Then he got out of the car.

He said, "Some more policemen are going to meet me here. I'll tell them about the man who said he was Mr. Fall's son. Then I'll take them with me to find out who he really is. We've got to find out what's going on here. We've got to find out who he really is."

"Do you think Mr. Fall is OK?" Tom asked.

"I hope so, Tom. But we won't know for sure before we see him. Try not to worry," Sergeant Collins said.

"Mr. Fall is our friend. We hope he is all right," Ricky said.

Sergeant Collins said, "Tell me again where he lives."

"In an old house across the street from Little's Stamp Store," Ricky said.

Just then two more police cars stopped in front of Eddie's house. Two policemen got out of the cars. Sergeant Collins walked over to talk with them. Then the two policemen got back in their cars.

Sergeant Collins walked back over to the boys. He said, "We're going to find out about Mr. Fall. I'll let you know how he is."

Two policemen got out of the cars. Sergeant Collins walked over to talk with them.

"Can we go with you?" Tom asked.

"No. It might not be safe. I don't want you to get hurt. You wait here," the Sergeant said.

Ricky said, "Can't we wait at the Stamp Store across from Mr. Fall's house?"

"All right. You can wait for me in front of the Stamp Store. But don't go to Mr. Fall's house before I tell you everything is OK," the Sergeant said.

"We won't," the three boys said.

Sergeant Collins got in his car and started down the street. The other two policemen went in their cars.

The three boys ran to their bikes. Patches ran with them.

Ricky said, "You stay here, Patches. You can't go with us. I'll come back for you soon."

The three boys got on their bikes and started after the policemen.

CHAPTER 8

Mr. Fall Is Helped

The boys went as fast as they could. Very soon they were at the Stamp Store. They got off their bikes and looked across the street at Mr. Fall's house. They saw Sergeant Collins walking up to Mr. Fall's front door. They didn't see the other policemen.

"Do you think that man will open the door?" Tom asked.

Ricky said, "I hope he does."

"We'll soon find out," Eddie said.

Sergeant Collins stood at Mr. Fall's front door for a long time. Then the boys heard something. It came from the back of the house. Sergeant Collins ran around to the back.

"What's going on? I hope everyone is all right," Tom said.

"I hope so, too," Ricky and Eddie both said.

A few minutes later the other policemen came around the house.

"I hope Sergeant Collins comes back outside with Mr. Fall," Tom said.

A few minutes later Sergeant Collins came outside. He had Mr. Fall with him. He called to the boys to come over to Mr. Fall's yard. They ran across the street.

Ricky said, "We sure are glad to see you, Mr. Fall."

"Are you all right?" Tom asked.

A few minutes later Sergeant Collins came outside. He had Mr. Fall with him.

"Thanks to you boys I am. I couldn't call for help. Those two men locked me in my room," Mr. Fall said.

Sergeant Collins said, "The men closed all of the windows. They wanted people to think no one was in the house. Then they could look at Little's Stamp Store. But no one would know it."

"Why were they looking at the store?" Tom asked.

"What's going on?" Eddie asked.

"They were waiting for the store to get in some very old stamps this afternoon. The stamps are worth a lot of money. We found out that the men were going to hold up the store and take the stamps," Sergeant Collins said.

Mr. Fall said, "Thank you for getting the police, boys. When the two men saw Sergeant Collins at the front door, they tried to run away. The other policemen were waiting for them outside the back door."

"You don't have to thank us, Mr. Fall. We did it because you are our friend. Do you still want us to help you clean out your garage?" Tom asked.

"Not today. I'm going to the police station now. I have to tell the police all about what the men did. Come back in a few days," Mr. Fall said.

"We sure will be back in a few days," Ricky said.

"Wait. How did you know that Australia has winter when we have summer?" Mr. Fall asked.

"I knew that, Mr. Fall. I read about it," Eddie said.

"I'm glad you knew about that. You saved my life. Australia is a fine place. The people are very nice. My real son likes it there a lot," Mr. Fall said.

Tom, Ricky, and Eddie got on their bikes. "Come on," Eddie called.

"Where are you going?" Ricky asked.

"I want to see those stamps," Eddie said.

"Let's go with him," Ricky said to Tom.

"OK," Tom said.

The boys pushed their bikes across the street. They locked the bikes and walked into the Stamp Store.

"Hi, Mr. Little," Ricky said.

"We would like to see those very old stamps," Tom said.

Eddie laughed. He said, "We sure would. Do you have any from Australia?"